Dear ... Baby-... Rockin'
Wishing you ... blessings
Birth da ...
Mamma
01. 01. 06

A catalogue record for this book is available from the British Library
Published by Ladybird Books Ltd
80 Strand London WC2R ORL
A Penguin Company

3 5 7 9 10 8 6 4

© LADYBIRD BOOKS MMIV

Animal Stories

Hissing Hattie

written by Melanie Joyce
illustrated by John Haslam

All through the jungle day, Hissing
Hattie wiggled and slithered
happily around the jungle
with her friends.

And every jungle night, she curled
herself into a neat spiral to go
to sleep.

But, one night, Hattie must have had very busy dreams. When she woke up in the morning, she had a big, fat knot in her tail.

"Oh no! Not a KNOT!" sighed Hattie.
She set off wiggling and slithering
through the jungle.

But the knot kept getting caught between roots and branches. Every time, Hattie jumped and jerked and hurt herself.

"Oh, bad luck! Not a KNOT!"
said Hattie's friend, Stripey Sam.
"When I've got a knot in my tail,
I twirl it round and round,
and twirl it out."

So Hattie tried twirling her tail but, oh no! She found she couldn't twirl her tail on its own. Her whole body twirled round and round until she grew dizzy.
"And the knot's still there," she sighed.

Hattie met her friend Huge Henry.
"Oh, bad luck! Not a KNOT!"
he trumpeted. "When I've got a knot in
my trunk, I go into the long tickly grass
and try to sneeze it out."

Henry showed Hattie the way
to the long tickly grass.

AAA-CHOO!

Soon, they were both sneezing away.

"And the knot's still...
AAA-CHOO!"
sneezed Hattie.

"No, thank you!" said Hattie,
slithering away as fast as
she could.

"It's no good," she said, sadly. "I'm stuck with this knot for ever and ever.

I'll just have to get used to it."

But Hattie's friends
hated to see her so unhappy.

"If we can't untangle Hattie's knot, let's have a jungle dance. At least then we can try to cheer her up," they said.

That evening, all the animals gathered to dance to the jungle music. Hattie forgot the knot as she slithered and swirled and twisted and twirled with her dancing partners, until suddenly...

"My Knot's gone!" she cried.
"Thank you, my friends!"

And then, under the jungle moon,
Hattie and her friends danced the
night away.